Jill's new bike

What Jill wanted was
   a new bike.
'Everyone in my class has a new
   bike but me,' she said, 'and my
   bike is so old.'

1

Jill lived with her mum at the
top of a big, old house.
One day Jill told her mum she
wanted a new bike.

Jill's mum looked sad.
'How can I pay for a new
   bike?' she said.
'It's a job to pay all the bills.'

Jill could see her mum was upset.
She gave her a kiss.
'Well, my old bike will do,' she said.

The next day, Jill went to see
  Mr and Mrs Hill.
The Hills lived on a small farm.
They liked Jill to call and see them.

Mrs Hill looked at Jill's old bike.
She could see Jill wanted a new one.
She said, 'How would you like to
do jobs on the farm?'

'Yes, we could do with a little help,'
said Mr Hill. 'Come back and
do a job every day.
We can pay you for all you do.'

Every day Jill went to the farm.
She helped Mr Hill stack logs.
She looked for eggs and helped
    Mrs Hill pack them on a rack.

She fed the hens and the cock.
They began to flap and cluck.
'Look how they peck,' said Jill, 'but I wish
    the cock wouldn't push so much.'

Jill helped Mrs Hill to feed
   a sick duck.
She helped Mr Hill muck out the pigs.
'What a smell!' said Jill.

The job Jill liked best of all was
to go for a run with Bess, the
farm dog.
'There's a lot to do on a farm,' she said.

Jill gave all her pay to her mum.
In the end, Mum sold Jill's old bike and
   got her a new one.
It was the one Jill wanted.

Mr Hill gave Jill a lock for the
    new bike.
'Don't forget to lock the bike up,'
    he told her.

One day, Jill went to the shops to
get some things for her mum.
She put her bike in the rack, but
she forgot to lock it.

When Jill got back to the bike rack, she couldn't see her bike.

'Oh no!' said Jill.

'The lock is still in my bag.'

Jill ran up to Mr Hill.
She began to cry.
'Don't cry,' he said. 'I took the bike.
It had no lock so I put it in my van.'

'I looked for you,' said Mr Hill, 'to
    tell you I had the bike.'
'It gave me a shock,' said Jill, 'but
    I won't forget to lock it next time.'

Pirates

'So you want to be like pirate men?'
   said Rod the Red and Peg Leg Ken.
'You want to be a pirate bold,
   like pirates were in days of old?

'We need a lad, there's lots to do,
   but do we need a lad like you?
You look too thin, you look too small.
You couldn't do the jobs at all.

Dust the cabins, rub the brass;
  sand the deck as flat as glass;
  fill up all the cracks with pitch;
  mend this canvas stitch by stitch.

'Cook the food and wash the socks;
see the ship around the rocks;
climb the mast when days are cold;
and help us dig up chests of gold.

'But if we see a speck of dust,
   a bit of fluff, a patch of rust,
   a spot of muck on cup or dish;
   we'll chuck you in to feed the fish.

'So could you be a pirate, then?'
said Rod the Red and Peg Leg Ken.
'We don't think you could, do you?'
'Oh yes, oh yes! You bet I do!'

What goes cluck?

What goes cluck, and what goes quack?
What goes hiss, and what barks back?
What goes clip-clop, what goes moo?
What goes, 'Well, well, how do you do?'